God is Good

God Made

the

Animals

By Mrs. James Swartzentruber

Pictures by Daniel Zook and Lester Miller

To the Teacher:

This book is designed to give constructive reading practice to pupils using the grade one *Bible Nurture and Reader Series.* It uses words that have been introduced in the reader or can be mastered with phonics skills taught by Unit 3, Lesson 15. A few new words also appear in the story, printed in italics. At the end of the book, these words are listed with pronunciations and / or illustrations to help the children to learn them on their own. Be sure the children understand that the words are vocabulary or sound words except the words in italics, and where to look to learn the new words if they need help. They should be able to read this book independently.

Books in this series with their placement according to reading and phonics lessons:

1. The Egg and the Chick   Unit 2, Lesson 30
2. The Squirrel and the Nut   Unit 3, Lesson 5
3. God Makes Seeds That Grow   Unit 3, Lesson 10
4. God Made the Animals   Unit 3, Lesson 15
5. God Made Me   Unit 3, Lesson 20
6. God Made Us   Unit 3, Lesson 25
7. We Should Be Thankful   Unit 3, Lesson 30
8. God Made the Opossum   Unit 4, Lesson 5
9. God Made the Firefly   Unit 4, Lesson 10

Printed in U.S.A.

ISBN 978-07399-0062-8

Catalog no. 2254

14   15   16   17   18   —   21   20   19   18   17   16   15   14   13   12

"Mother, may June and I go
back to the creek?" asked James.
"We are finished with the
weeds."

3

"Fine," said Mother. "What did you do with them?"

"We put most of them in the ditch, but we gave some to the hens," said James.

"That is good. The hens could have had all of them. Green things are good for hens. But that is all right.

"You have worked hard. You may go to the creek for a while. Be back in time for *supper*," said Mother.

"Oh, thank you, Mother!" cried the twins.

On the way to the creek,
James and June went past the
hens. "Look!" said June. "They
ate all those weeds!"

"Let's get the weeds in the ditch and give them to the hens, too," said James.

The twins ran to the ditch. James picked up as many as he could. "Put some more on top of this," he said.

June gave James some more weeds. "Do you want more than that?" she asked him.

"A few more," said James.

June put on a few more.

"Stop. I think that is about all I can take," said James.

When James came back for more weeds, he saw something

move in the grass. He went close.
He looked.

"What do you see, James?"
called June.

"Come and see," said James.

June came and looked. She saw it, too. It was a nest. It was a nest that had little baby *bunnies* in it!

"Oh, let's go away," said June, "or the *bunnies* may run out and get lost."

"We did not see this nest in all the time we took weeds to the ditch!" said James.

As the twins went on to the creek, they talked about the nest. "The mother hid that very well," said James. "We walked past that place many times but did not see it. We could have stepped on her *bunnies* because we did not see the nest."

"Oh!" squealed June, as a *rabbit* dashed away from her feet. "I just about stepped on that *rabbit*! It was sitting so still that I did not see it."

"There must be many *rabbits* around here," said James. "How can they know so much? How did that mother *rabbit* know how to hide her nest? What made this one sit so still that we could not see it was there?"

Soon they came to the creek.

"The water is not very deep

today," said James when they stepped into the water. "But it is nice and cool. It feels good."

The twins had fun playing in the water. They liked to make it splash.

There were little fish in the water. June and James tried to catch one but they could not. The fish could swim so fast that it was hard to see where they went.

"How can such little things *move* so fast?" June asked.

"I do not know," said James. "I cannot *move* that fast!"

"It will soon be time to eat. Maybe we should go," said June.

"Oh, look at that pretty bird!" said James, pointing to a bird beside the path as they started home. "It is dragging its wing. It cannot fly."

"It is hurt!" cried June.

"Let's catch it and take it home," said James. "Maybe

Father can fix its wing."

The twins ran to catch the bird. When they were quite close,

James put his hands down to get
it, but the bird hopped out of his
reach. He tried again and again,
but the bird kept hopping away,
always just out of reach.

At last James made one big
jump to grab the bird. This time
it did not hop away. This time it
lifted the dragging wing and flew.

"Oh!" said June.

"Oh!" said James.

They watched the bird go up, up, up. It flew far away. It was not hurt at all.

"Why did it do that?" asked June.

"I do not know," said James. "I did not think it could fly. It played a trick on us. We have many things to tell Father and Mother. Come, let us go home."

When Mother saw James and June, she said, "Good. It will soon be time to eat. I need you to help me."

The twins helped Mother.
Soon Father came. While they
were eating *supper*, the twins told

their parents what they had seen.

"We did not think the bird could fly!" said June. "We tried to catch it to bring it home, but we could not. It flew away!"

Father and Mother smiled. Father said, "The bird had a nest close by. It acted hurt so that you would run after it and get far away from the nest. It knew what to do to get you away from its nest."

"Oh!" said James.

"Oh!" said June.

"God made the bird to know

what to do so that it could keep its family safe," said Mother. "Many animals would like to find a nest of little birds to eat. The mother knows how to lead them away from the nest."

"So that is why it did that!" said James. "Did God make the *rabbit* to know how to hide its nest, too?"

"And to sit still?" asked June. "I just about stepped on one!"

"Yes," said Father. "God helps them to make a nest so that

it is hard to see. A fox or a dog
would like to eat little *bunnies*.
The mother *rabbit* makes her
nest look like the grass. That way

other animals cannot see it very well."

"We saw a nest where a *rabbit* did that," James said. "We went right past it every time we took some weeds there. But we did not see it for a long time."

"And then when we were going to the creek," said June, "a *rabbit* jumped out right at my feet. I just about stepped on it."

"She squealed." James smiled.

"I did not expect to see a *rabbit* right then." June smiled back.

Mother said, "If you had not been so close, it may have stayed where it was and never *moved* at all. And you would never have known that it was there."

"It is a good thing God made the animals like that," said James.

"Yes, it is," said Father. "God made the animals in a good way. He helps them to know what to do to keep safe. Everything He made is very good."

supper (sup·ėr)

move (mo͞ov)

rabbits (rab·its)

bunnies (bun·ēz)

moved (mo͞ovd)

lost (lôst)